Fat mother cat was asleep on her mat.

Said her four little kittens,
"There's no fun in that!"
And they went off round the farm to run wild.

Said the marmalade kitten,
spiking her claws,
"I am a terrible tiger!
I shall hunt hen out of her hutch."

And she tried to growl
(But she didn't know how)
She could only go . . .

miaow miaow

And hen went

CLUCK
CLUCK
CLUCK

Said the black little kitten,
with a glint in his eye,
"I am a panther on the prowl.
I shall frighten pig out of his sty."

And he tried to howl
(But he didn't know how)
He could only go . . .

And pig went

OINK OINK OINK

Said the tortoiseshell kitten,
pricking her ears,
"I am a leaping leopard!
I shall chase duck into her pond."

And she tried to snarl
(But she didn't know how)
She could only go . . .

miaow miaow

And duck went
QUACK QUACK QUACK

Said the tabby little kitten, twitching her tail,
"I am a dangerous lion!
I shall make the sheep run down the lane."

And she tried to roar
(But she didn't know how)
She could only go . . .

miaow

miaow

And the sheep went
BAA BAA BAA

Said the four little kittens, ever so fierce,
"We are tigers! Panthers! Leopards! Lions!
We shall scare that gaggle of geese!"

And they tried to roar,
To snarl, to growl,
And they managed to go . . .

miaow! miaow!

But the geese went

HONK

HONK

HONK

Then a puppy came over to play.

Those four fierce kittens arched their backs.
Their fur stood on end. They hissed. They spat!
And that terrified puppy ran away . . .

Said those proud little kittens,
"We didn't know we could do THAT!"

And they went back to their mother,
to sleep on the mat.